Yeti Loves Spaghetti has been a long labor of love, starting with a handmade plush Yeti and slowly spinning into this story over the years.

Thank you for buying an authorized copy of this book and for complying with copyright laws by not reproducing, scanning or distributing any part of it in any form without permission from the author.

No part of this publication may be reproduced, stored in a retrieval system, or transmitted in any form or by any means, electronic, mechanical, photocopying, recording, or otherwise, without written permission of the author.

IBSN 978-1-7378706-9-2

Text and illustration copyright © 2024 by Breia Mallett
All rights reserved.

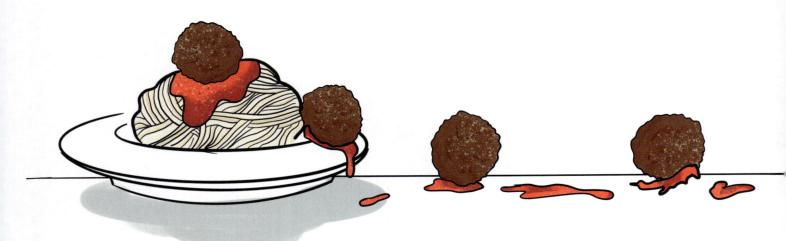

This is my friend, Harry.
He's a pretty furry dude.

Anatomy of a Yeti

horns

Essential Spaghetti eating tools

fluffy

White fur

Claws

He is white and he is fluffy

And he loves one messy food!

(other types of monsters)

YETI

Though Harry is a monster...

(More specifically a yeti)

His favorite messy food
is a big bowl of spaghetti!

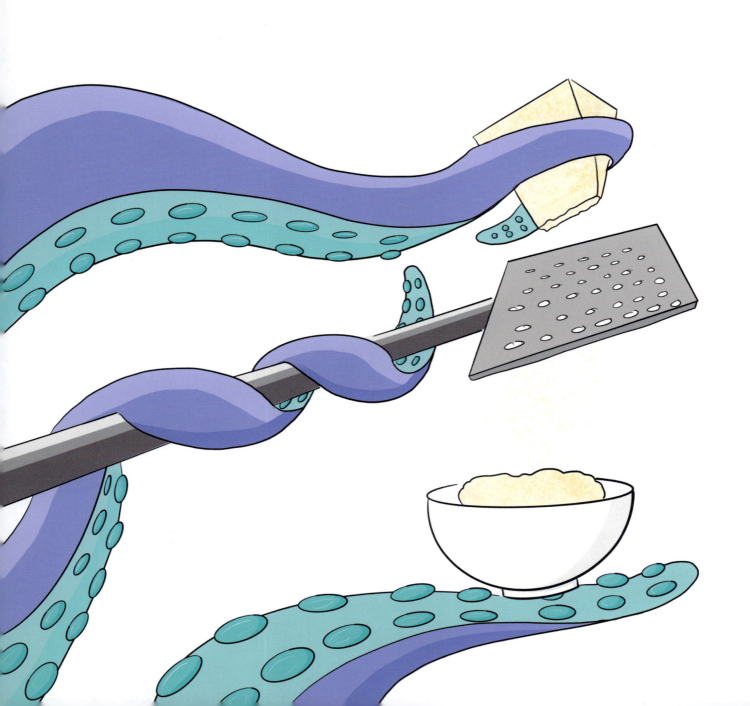

Freshly shaved Parmesan,
a salty pile of cheese.

Harry, the furry yeti, begs

Would you add some more?
PLEASE!!!

Now here is Harry's quandary: his fur is snowy white.

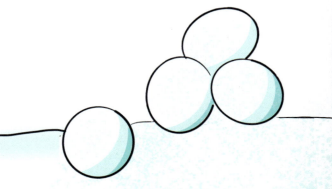

And he loves to eat
this messy food
most every single night.

Despite his best intentions of staying nice and clean,

One thing that isn't tidy is his favorite-ist cuisine!

So, Harry thought and thought.

and thought, and thought, and thought...

His first try was a rubber bib to keep from getting stained.

But, the cheese and sauce slid right down...
That mess was NOT contained!

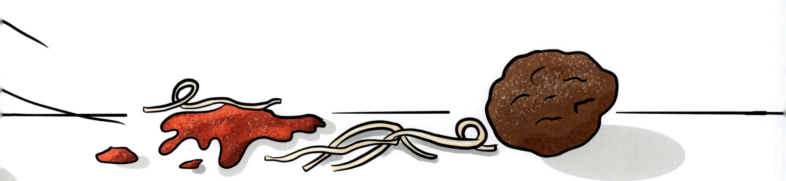

Harry did not give up though.
Back to the drawing board he went.

A fail proof way to keep him clean is what he would invent!

He worked his crafty Yeti claws and fashioned up a smock.

But, it came out way
too small and the
sauce it did not block.

So he decided to take a walk before throwing in the towel.

But; when he glanced out the front door the weather just looked foul.

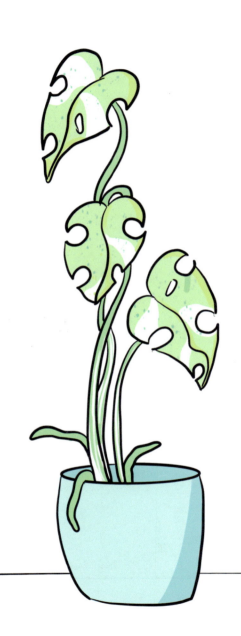

Harry reached for his umbrella to keep from getting wet.

It was at this very moment that he had his best idea yet!

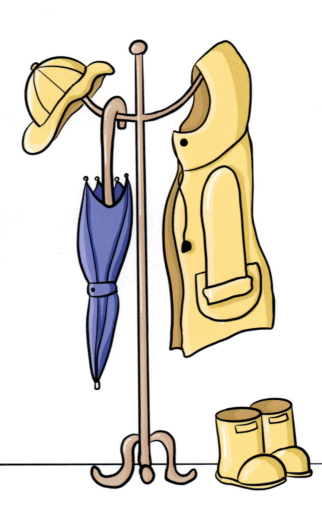

Now my good friend Harry,
that white and fluffy dude,
no longer has to worry
when he eats his favorite food!

HI! My name is BREIA

and I am the author and doodler of this book.

Harry came about after I sewed my daughter, Marjorie, a fluffy Yeti stuffie to help her see that the "monsters" in her closet were just cute, loveable floofs who were nothing to be scared of. I would tell her tales of Harry's life such as where he lived, his favorite foods, what he did for fun, etc. As I know you also now know, his favorite food is spaghetti and the tale just grew from there.

A long time drawer of cute little doodles, I got to work creating a visual world for Harry and his saucy adventures and that's how we got where we are today.

I live in the beautiful Pacific Northwest with my family, just north of Seattle in a town called Edmonds, WA. When I'm not spending time with said family, you can find me drawing, sewing, crafting, creating and tinkering. Sometimes the family time also involves one or more of the above activities too!

Thank you so much for reading my silly little tale, sharing this story with you means the world to me.

Made in United States
Troutdale, OR
12/23/2024